The Thunderstruck Stork

David J. Olson

Illustrated by Lynn Munsinger

ALBERT WHITMAN & COMPANY, MORTON GROVE, ILLINOIS

To my Gramma and Grampa.—D.J.O.

Library of Congress Cataloging-in-Publication Data

Olson, David (David James)
The thunderstruck stork / by David J. Olson ; illustrated by Lynn Munsinger.
p. cm.
Summary: When Webster the stork collides with a hot air balloon and his brain is knocked out of whack,
he starts delivering the wrong babies to animal parents all over the world, with surprising results.
ISBN 10: 0-8075-7910-6 (hardcover)   ISBN 13: 978-0-8075-7910-7 (hardcover)
[1. Animals—Fiction. 2. Animals—Infancy—Fiction. 3. Storks—Fiction.
4. Humorous stories. 5. Stories in rhyme.] I. Munsinger, Lynn, ill. II. Title.
PZ8.3.O498Th 2007 [E]—dc22 2007001505

Text copyright © 2007 by David J. Olson.
Illustrations copyright © 2007 by Lynn Munsinger.
Published in 2007 by Albert Whitman & Company, 6340 Oakton Street, Morton Grove, Illinois 60053-2723.
Published simultaneously in Canada by Fitzhenry & Whiteside, Markham, Ontario.
Printed in China through Colorcraft Ltd., Hong Kong.
10 9 8 7 6 5 4 3 2 1

The design is by Carol Gildar.

For more information about Albert Whitman & Company,
please visit our web site at www.albertwhitman.com.

All the new babies west of New York
were delivered by Webster, the white-feathered stork.
Webster had never, not ever gone wrong—
until the strange eve of May first came along.

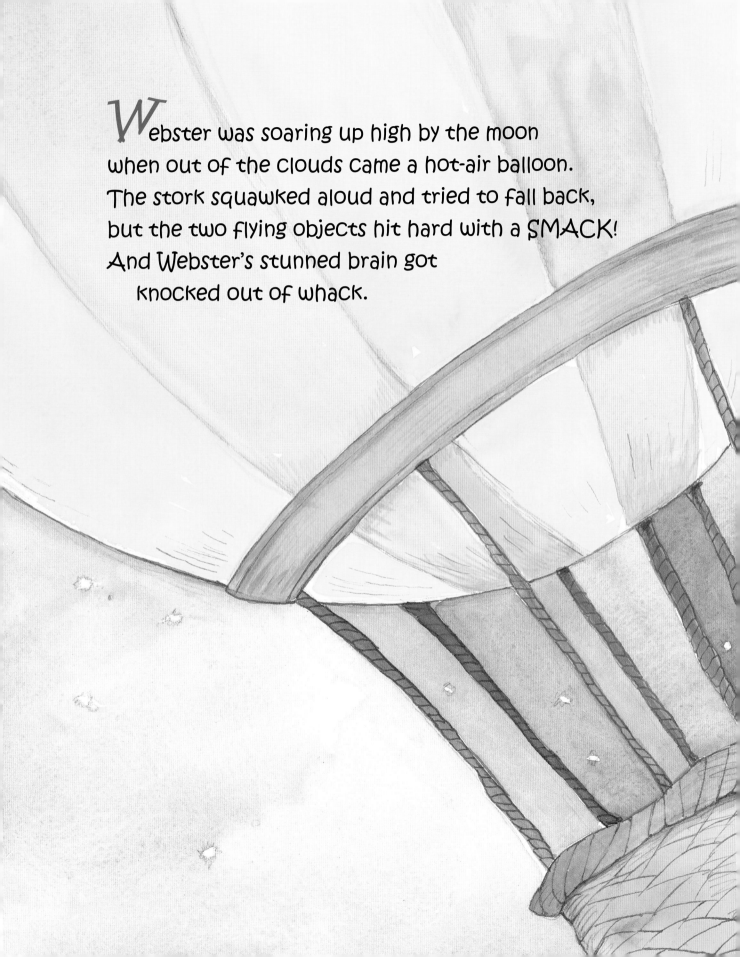

Webster was soaring up high by the moon
when out of the clouds came a hot-air balloon.
The stork squawked aloud and tried to fall back,
but the two flying objects hit hard with a SMACK!
And Webster's stunned brain got
knocked out of whack.

The following Sunday, seven days later,
deep in the Swamp of the Giggling Gator,
two anxious frogs sat waiting around
for their newly born baby to float to the ground.

The parents-to-be turned their eyes
to the sky,
watching for Webster the stork to fly by.

The bird dropped a package all bundled in white,
attached to a parachute slowing its flight.

They quickly unfastened the small safety pin,
and gaped at the odd-looking baby within.
The kid was *enormous*—gigantic and tall.
His body was bulky, not small, not at all.

His ears were as big as a ship's flapping sails,
and his skin was as gray as rain clouds and nails.
And his nose, I believe it's important to note,
hung down past his lips and his chin and his throat!

The two Ribberts gasped, and their eyeballs bulged out.
Dad said, "He's somewhat peculiar, no doubt.
He's not like the rest of the frogs that we know,
but Honey, he's ours, and we'll cherish him so."

Meanwhile, high in the trees of Old Twig,
a family of sparrows received a young pig.
"Good-bye!" Webster cried to the pleased mother bird,
but the sparrows soon questioned the oinks that
   they heard.

The sharks in Blue Bay
were deeply love-stricken
when Webster delivered
a chirping new chicken.

The bats in the barn
were delivered a moose,

and the lions down south
got a well-mannered goose.

Spiders got monkeys with long curly tails,
and a hamster dropped down to a family of whales.

Giraffes received hippos,
and hippos got bears,

but the parents adored them
because they were theirs!

The sharks taught their
sweet peeping chicken to swim
with goggles and snorkels
while tied to Mom's fin.

The eight-legged spiders
spun gray spider lines
so their monkey could swing
on his own wispy "vines."

From his antlers, the moose
let his bat parents cling,
and he'd rock *them* to sleep
with his head as a swing.

The birds pushed their piglet right out of the nest
to teach him to fly—a difficult test.
The poor pig hit the ground with a tear in his eye,
for everyone knows that piglets can't fly.

The sparrows decided that come the next spring,
they'd help the pig fly with balloons and some string.

These uncommon families were having a ball,
and soon they forgot they were mixed up at all.

And then something happened.
From out of the blue,
a thunderstorm squall
was beginning to brew.

From high in the sky there came a bright FLASH,
along with a booming and ear-splitting CRASH!
A streak of white lightning pierced through the air,
and ZAPPED the poor stork, who was soaring up there.

The hot bolt of lightning straightened him out—
his circuits were no longer scrambled about.
The stork hung his head and cried, "WHAT HAVE I DONE?
I'm seven times worse than Attila the Hun!

"I have to correct this incredible mess,
but I'll need some help," the bird had to confess.
He took a deep breath down into his chest,
shook his burnt feathers, and headed out west.

Two mornings later, at seven-oh-nine,
just as the sun was beginning to shine,
something appeared in the pink morning light—
a tremendous, amazing, remarkable sight.

Ten thousand storks were fluttering in,
to help put the world back to normal again!

They came from Los Angeles, France, and New York,
and leading the army was Webster the stork!
"Don't worry!" he hollered with all of his might.
"I'm back with my friends to make everything right!"

But just before Webster commanded his band
to swap all the babies across the vast land,
he spotted a caring and kind mother squirrel
carefully feeding her baby frog girl.

Not far away was a father baboon,
climbing a tree with his baby raccoon.
And the rabbits that lived on the
green, grassy knoll
were hugging and kissing their
fuzzy-faced mole.

The thunderstruck bird stopped short in mid-flight,
for suddenly Webster the stork saw the light—
the babies were switched up as switched up
      could be,
yet still they were treasured—like you
      and like me!

The stork told the ten thousand birds to go home,
and left all the jumbled-up babies alone.
Webster's big heart beat proud in his chest.
He knew that the families he'd made were the BEST!